OTHER BOOKS BY JEFF KINNEY

Diary of a Wimpy Kid

Diary of a Wimpy Kid: Rodrick Rules

Diary of a Wimpy Kid: The Last Straw

Diary of a Wimpy Kid: The Ugly Truth

Diary of a Wimpy Kid Do-It-Yourself Book

The Wimpy Kid Movie Diary

COMING SOON

More *Diary of a Wimpy Kid*

DIARY
of a
Wimpy Kid
DOG DAYS

by Jeff Kinney

AMULET BOOKS
New York

The Library of Congress has cataloged
the hardcover edition of this book as follows:

Kinney, Jeff.
Diary of a wimpy kid : dog days / by Jeff Kinney.
p. cm.
Summary: In the latest diary of middle-schooler Greg Heffley, he records his attempts to spend his summer vacation sensibly indoors playing video games and watching television, despite his mother's other ideas.
ISBN 978-0-8109-8391-5 (Harry N. Abrams)
[1. Summer—Fiction. 2. Diaries—Fiction. 3. Humorous stories.] I. Title. II.
Title: Diary of a wimpy kid four.
PZ7.K6232Di 2009
[Fic]—dc22
2009024953

International edition ISBN 978-0-8109-9751-6

Book design by Jeff Kinney
Cover design by Chad W. Beckerman and Jeff Kinney

Printed and bound in U.S.A.
13 12 11 10 9 8 7 6 5 4

ABRAMS
THE ART OF BOOKS SINCE 1949
115 West 18th Street
New York, NY 10011
www.abramsbooks.com

TO JONATHAN

<u>Friday</u>

For me, summer vacation is basically a three-month guilt trip.

Just because the weather's nice, everyone expects you to be outside all day "frolicking" or whatever. And if you don't spend every second outdoors, people think there's something wrong with you. But the truth is, I've always been more of an indoor person.

The way I like to spend my summer vacation is in front of the TV, playing video games with the curtains closed and the lights turned off.

Unfortunately, Mom's idea of the perfect summer vacation is different from mine.

Mom says it's not "natural" for a kid to stay indoors when it's sunny out. I tell her that I'm just trying to protect my skin so I don't look all wrinkly when I'm old like her, but she doesn't want to hear it.

Mom keeps trying to get me to do something outside, like go to the pool. But I spent the first part of the summer at my friend Rowley's pool, and that didn't work out so good.

Rowley's family belongs to a country club, and when school let out for the summer, we were going there every single day.

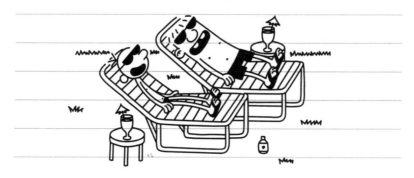

Then we made the mistake of inviting this girl named Trista who just moved into our neighborhood. I thought it would be really nice of us to share our country club lifestyle with her. But five seconds after we got to the pool, she met some lifeguard and forgot all about the guys who invited her there.

The lesson I learned is that some people won't think twice about using you, especially when there's a country club involved.

Me and Rowley were better off without a girl hanging around, anyway. We're both bachelors at the moment, and during the summer it's better to be unattached.

A few days ago I noticed the quality of service at the country club was starting to go down a little. Like sometimes the temperature in the sauna was a few degrees too hot, and one time the poolside waiter forgot to put one of those little umbrellas in my fruit smoothie.

I reported all my complaints to Rowley's dad. But for some reason Mr. Jefferson never passed them on to the clubhouse manager.

Which is kind of weird. If it was me who was paying for a country club membership, I'd want to make sure I was getting my money's worth.

Anyway, a little while later Rowley told me he wasn't allowed to invite me to his pool anymore, which is fine with ME. I'm much happier inside my air-conditioned house, where I don't have to check my soda can for bees every time I go to take a sip.

Like I said, Mom keeps trying to get me to go to the pool with her and my little brother, Manny, but the thing is, my family belongs to the TOWN pool, not the country club. And once you've tasted the country club life, it's hard to go back to being an ordinary Joe at the town pool.

Besides, last year I swore to myself that I would never go back to that place again. At the town pool you have to go through the locker room before you can go swimming, and that means walking through the shower area, where grown men are soaping down right out in the open.

The first time I walked through the men's locker room at the town pool was one of the most traumatic experiences of my life.

I'm probably lucky I didn't go blind. Seriously, I don't see why Mom and Dad bother to try and protect me from horror movies and stuff like that if they're gonna expose me to something about a thousand times worse.

I really wish Mom would stop asking me to go to the town pool, because every time she does, it puts images in my mind that I've been trying hard to forget.

<u>Sunday</u>

Well, now I'm DEFINITELY staying indoors
for the rest of the summer. Mom had a "house
meeting" last night and said money is tight this
year and we can't afford to go to the beach,
which means no family vacation.

THAT really stinks. I was actually looking
FORWARD to going to the beach this summer.
Not because I like the ocean and the sand and
all of that, because I don't. I realized a long
time ago that all the world's fish and turtles and
whales go to the bathroom right there in the
ocean. And I seem to be the only person who's
bothered by this.

My brother Rodrick likes to tease me because he thinks I'm afraid of the waves. But I'm telling you, that's not it at all.

Anyway, I was looking forward to going to the beach because I'm finally tall enough to go on the Cranium Shaker, which is this really awesome ride that's on the boardwalk. Rodrick's been on the Cranium Shaker at least a hundred times, and he says you can't call yourself a man until you ride it.

Mom said maybe if we "save our pennies" we can go back to the beach next year. Then she said we'd still do a lot of fun stuff as a family and one day we'll look back on this as the "best summer ever."

Well, now I only have two things to look forward to this summer. One is my birthday, and the other is when the last "Li'l Cutie" comic runs in the paper. I don't know if I ever mentioned this before, but "Li'l Cutie" is the worst comic ever. To give you an idea of what I'm talking about, here's what ran in the paper today —

Daddy, is rain just God sweating?

But here's the thing: Even though I hate "Li'l Cutie," I can't stop myself from reading it, and Dad can't, either. I guess we just like seeing how bad it is.

"Li'l Cutie" has been around for at least thirty years, and it's written by this guy named Bob Post. I've heard Li'l Cutie is based on Bob's son when he was a little kid.

But I guess now that the real Li'l Cutie is all grown up, his dad's having trouble coming up with new material.

A couple of weeks ago the newspaper announced that Bob Post is retiring and the final "Li'l Cutie" is gonna be printed in August. Ever since then me and Dad have been counting down the days until the last comic runs.

When the last "Li'l Cutie" comes out, me and Dad will have to throw a party, because something like that deserves a serious celebration.

Monday

Even though me and Dad see eye to eye on "Li'l Cutie," there are still a lot of things we butt heads over. The big issue between us right now is my sleep schedule. During the summer I like to stay up all night watching TV or playing video games and then sleep through the morning. But Dad gets kind of crabby if I'm still in bed when he gets home from work.

Lately, Dad's been calling me at noon to make sure I'm not still asleep. So I keep a phone by my bed and use my best wide-awake voice when he calls.

I think Dad's jealous because he has to go to work while the rest of us get to kick back and take it easy every day.

But if he's gonna be all grumpy about it, he should just become a teacher or a snowplow driver or have one of those jobs where you get to take summers off.

Mom's not really helping improve Dad's mood, either. She calls him at work about five times a day with updates on everything that's going on around the house.

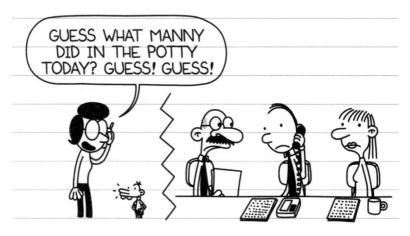

Tuesday
Dad got Mom a new camera for Mother's Day, and lately she's been taking lots of pictures. I think it's because she feels guilty about not keeping up on the family photo albums.

When my older brother, Rodrick, was a baby, Mom was totally on top of things.

Rodrick's first time trying peas

Rodrick's second time trying peas

Rodrick's first steps

Kaboom!

Once I came along I guess Mom got busy, so from that point on there are a lot of gaps in our official family history.

Welcome Gregory
to the world

Taking Gregory home
from the hospital

Gregory's 6th
birthday party

Gregory's first
day of middle school

I've learned that photo albums aren't an accurate
record of what happened in your life, anyway.
Last year when we were at the beach, Mom
bought a bunch of fancy seashells at a gift shop,
and later on I saw her bury them in the sand
for Manny to "discover."

Well, I wish I didn't see that, because it made me re-evaluate my whole childhood.

Gregory really "digs" seashells!

Today Mom said I was looking "shaggy," so she told me she was taking me to get a haircut.

But I never would've agreed to get my hair cut if I knew that Mom was taking me to Bombshells Beauty Salon, which is where Mom and Gramma get THEIR hair cut.

I have to say, though, the whole beauty salon experience wasn't that bad. First of all, they have TVs all over the place, so you can watch a show while you're waiting to get your hair cut.

Second, they have lots of tabloids, those newspapers you see in the checkout lines at grocery stores. Mom says tabloids are full of lies, but I think there's some really important stuff in those things.

Gramma is always buying tabloids, even though Mom doesn't approve. A few weeks ago Gramma wasn't answering her phone, so Mom got worried and drove over to Gramma's to see if she was OK. Gramma was fine, but she wasn't picking up her phone because of something she read.

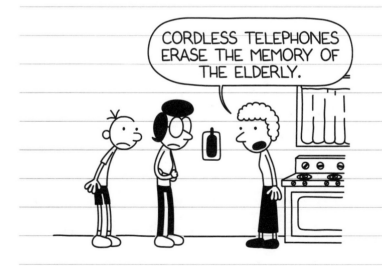

But when Mom asked Gramma where she got her information, Gramma said —

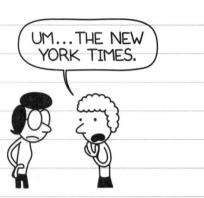

UM... THE NEW YORK TIMES.

Gramma's dog, Henry, died recently, and ever since then Gramma has had a lot of time on her hands. So Mom's dealing with stuff like the cordless phone thing a lot these days.

Whenever Mom finds any tabloids at Gramma's house, she takes them home and throws them in the garbage. Last week I fished one out of the trash and read it in my bedroom.

I'm glad I did. I found out that North America will be underwater within six months, so that kind of takes the pressure off me to do well in school.

I had a long wait at the beauty salon, but I didn't really mind. I got to read my horoscope and look at pictures of movie stars without their makeup, so I was definitely entertained.

When I got my hair cut, I found out the best thing about the beauty salon, which is the GOSSIP. The ladies who work there know the dirt on just about everyone in town.

...AND THEN MARLENE SAYS TO VANESSA, "IF YOU'RE GONNA GET UP IN MY FACE, YOU'D BETTER BE READY TO BACK IT UP!"

MM MM MM.

Unfortunately, Mom came to pick me up right in the middle of a story about Mr. Peppers and his new wife, who's twenty years younger than him.

Hopefully my hair will grow out fast so I can come back and hear the rest of the story.

Friday
I think Mom's starting to regret taking me to get my hair cut the other day. The ladies at Bombshells introduced me to soap operas, and now I'm totally hooked.

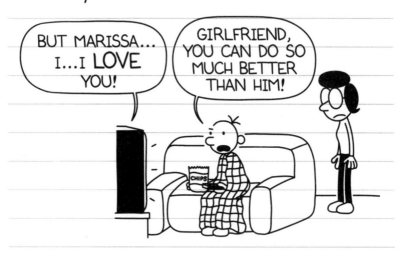

Yesterday I was in the middle of my show, and Mom told me I had to turn off the TV and find something else to do. I could tell there was no use arguing with her, so I called Rowley and invited him over.

When Rowley got to my house, we went straight to Rodrick's room in the basement. Rodrick is off playing with his band, Löded Diper, and whenever he's away I like to go through his stuff and see if I can find anything interesting.

The best thing I found in Rodrick's junk drawer this time around was one of those little souvenir picture keychains you get at the beach.

If you look into it, you see a picture of Rodrick with some girl.

I don't know how Rodrick got that picture, because I've been with him on every single family vacation, and if I saw him with THAT girl, I definitely would have remembered her.

I showed the picture to Rowley, but I had to hold the keychain because he was getting all grabby.

We dug around some more, and then we found a
horror movie at the bottom of Rodrick's drawer.
I couldn't believe our luck. Neither one of us had
actually seen a horror movie before, so this was a
really big find.

I asked Mom if Rowley could spend the night,
and she said yes. I made sure I asked Mom when
Dad was out of the room, because Dad doesn't
like it when I have sleepovers on a "work night."

Last summer Rowley spent the night at my
house, and we slept in the basement.

I made sure Rowley took the bed that was closest to the furnace room, because that room really freaks me out. I figured if anything came out of there in the middle of the night, it would grab Rowley first and I'd have a five-second head start to escape.

At about 1:00 in the morning, we heard something in the furnace room that scared the living daylights out of us.

It sounded like a little ghost girl or something, and it said —

Me and Rowley practically trampled each other to death trying to get up the basement stairs.

We burst into Mom and Dad's room, and I told them our house was haunted and we had to move immediately.

Dad didn't seem convinced, and he went down to the basement and walked right into the furnace room. Me and Rowley stayed about ten feet back.

I was pretty sure Dad wasn't going to get out of there alive. I heard some rustling and a few bumps, and I was ready to make a run for it.

THUNK
WHUMP

But a few seconds later he came back out with one
of Manny's toys, a doll named Hide-and-Seek Harry.

Last night me and Rowley waited for Mom and
Dad to go to bed, and then we watched our
movie. Technically, I was the only one who
watched it, because Rowley had his eyes and ears
covered the whole entire time.

The movie was about this muddy hand that goes around the country killing people. And the last person who sees the hand is always the next victim.

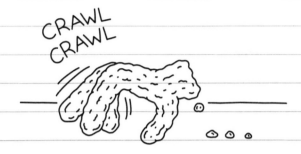

The special effects were really cheesy, and I wasn't even scared until the very end. That's when the twist came.

After the muddy hand strangled its last victim, it came crawling straight at the screen, and then the screen went black. At first I was a little confused, but then I realized it meant the next victim was gonna be ME.

I turned the TV off, and then I described the whole movie to Rowley from beginning to end.

Well, I must've done a pretty good job telling the story, because Rowley got even more freaked-out than I was.

I knew we couldn't go to Mom and Dad this time because they'd ground me if they found out we watched a horror movie. But we didn't feel safe in the basement, so we spent the rest of the night in the upstairs bathroom with the lights on.

I just wish we had managed to stay awake the whole night, because when Dad found us in the morning, it wasn't a pretty scene.

Dad wanted to know what was going on, and I had to fess up. Dad told Mom, so now I'm just waiting to hear how long I'm gonna be grounded for. But to be honest with you, I'm a lot more worried about this muddy hand than any punishment Mom can dream up.

I thought about it, though, and I realized there's only so much ground a muddy hand can cover in a day.

So hopefully that means I have a little while longer to live.

Tuesday

Yesterday, Mom lectured me about how boys my age watch too many violent movies and play too many video games, and that we don't know what REAL entertainment is.

I just stayed quiet, because I wasn't sure exactly where she was going with all this.

Then Mom said that she was gonna start a "reading club" for the boys in the neighborhood so she could teach us about all the great literature we were missing out on.

I begged Mom to just give me a regular punishment instead, but she wouldn't budge.

So today was the first meeting of the Reading Is Fun Club. I felt kind of bad for all the boys whose moms made THEM come.

I was just glad Mom didn't invite Fregley, this weird kid who lives up the street, because he's been acting stranger than usual lately.

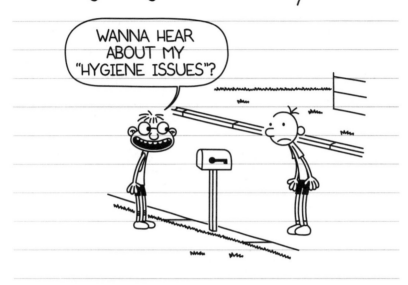

I'm starting to think maybe Fregley's a little dangerous, but luckily he doesn't really leave his front yard during the summer. I think his parents must have an electrical fence or something.

Anyway, Mom told everyone to bring their favorite book to today's meeting so we could pick one and discuss it. All the guys laid their books on the table, and everyone seemed pretty happy with the selection except Mom.

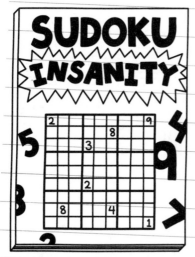

Mom said the books we brought weren't "real" literature and that we were gonna have to start with the "classics."

Then she brought out a bunch of books that she must've had since SHE was a kid.

These are the exact same types of books our teachers are always pushing us to read at school.

They have a program where if you read a "classic" in your free time, they reward you with a sticker of a hamburger or something like that.

I don't know who they think they're fooling. You can get a sheet of a hundred stickers down at the arts-and-crafts store for fifty cents.

I'm not really sure what makes a book a "classic" to begin with, but I think it has to be at least fifty years old and some person or animal has to die at the end.

Mom said if we didn't like the books she picked out, we could go on a field trip to the library and find something we all agreed on. But that won't work for me.

See, when I was eight years old I borrowed a book from the library, and then I forgot all about it. I found the book a few years later behind my desk, and I figured I must've owed about two thousand dollars in late fees on that thing.

So I buried the book in a box of old comics in my closet, and that's where it is to this day. I haven't been back to the library since then, but I know if I ever DO show up, they'll be waiting for me.

GREG HEFFLEY, YOU ARE UNDER ARREST FOR FAILING TO RETURN "HOW TO MAKE SOCK PUPPETS."

In fact, I get nervous if I even SEE a librarian.

I asked Mom if we could get a second chance to pick out a book on our own, and she said we could. We're supposed to meet again tomorrow and bring our new selections with us.

Wednesday
Well, the membership of the Reading Is Fun Club took a big hit overnight. Most of the guys who came yesterday bailed out, and now there's only two of us.

Rowley brought two books along with him.

The book I picked was the ninth volume in the "Magick and Monsters: Dark Realms" series. I figured Mom would like it because it's pretty long and there aren't any pictures.

But Mom didn't like my book. She said she didn't approve of the illustration on the cover because she didn't like the way it portrayed women.

I've read "Shadowdoom," and from what I can remember, there aren't even any women in the story. In fact, I kind of wonder if the person who designed the cover even READ the book.

Anyway, Mom said that she was gonna use her veto power as the Reading Is Fun Club's founder and choose the book for us. So she chose this book called "Charlotte's Web," which looks like one of those "classics" I was talking about before.

Just from looking at the cover, I guarantee either the girl or the pig doesn't make it to the end of the book.

Friday
Well, the Reading Is Fun Club is down to one member, and that's me.

Yesterday Rowley went golfing or something with his dad, so he kind of hung me out to dry. I didn't do my reading assignment, and I was really counting on him to cover for me at the meeting.

It's not really my fault that I couldn't finish my reading assignment, though. Mom told me I had to read in my bedroom for twenty minutes yesterday, but the truth is, I just have trouble concentrating for long periods of time.

After Mom caught me horsing around, she
banned me from watching TV until I read the
book. So last night I had to wait until she went
to bed before I could get my entertainment fix.

I kept thinking about that movie with the muddy
hand, though. I was afraid that if I was watching
TV all by myself late at night, the muddy hand
might crawl out from under the couch and grab my
foot or something.

The way I solved the problem was by making a
trail of clothes and other stuff all the way from my
bedroom down to the family room.

That way I was able to make it downstairs and back without ever touching the ground.

This morning Dad tripped over a dictionary I left at the top of the stairs, so now he's mad at me. But I'll take Dad being angry over the alternative any day of the week.

My new fear is that the hand is gonna crawl up on my bed and get me in my sleep. So lately I've been covering my whole body with the blanket and leaving a hole so I can breathe.

But that strategy has its OWN risks. Rodrick got into my room today, and I had to spend the morning trying to wash the taste of a dirty sock out of my mouth.

Sunday

Today was my deadline for finishing the first three chapters of "Charlotte's Web." When Mom found out I wasn't done yet, she said we were gonna sit down at the kitchen table until I was finished.

About a half hour later there was a knock at
the front door, and it was Rowley. I thought
maybe he was coming back to the Reading Is
Fun Club, but when I saw that his dad was with
him, I knew something was up.

Mr. Jefferson had an official-looking piece of
paper with the country club logo on it. He said it
was a bill for all the fruit smoothies me and
Rowley ordered at the clubhouse, and the grand
total was eighty-three dollars.

All those times me and Rowley ordered drinks at
the clubhouse, we just wrote down Mr. Jefferson's
account number on the tab. Nobody told us someone
actually had to PAY for all that.

I still didn't really understand what Mr. Jefferson was doing at MY house. I think he's an architect or something, so if he needs eighty-three bucks, he can just design an extra building. He talked to Mom, though, and they both agreed that me and Rowley needed to pay off the tab.

I told Mom me and Rowley are just kids and it's not like we have salaries or careers or whatever. But Mom said we were just gonna have to be "creative." Then she said we would have to suspend the Reading Is Fun Club's meetings until we paid what we owed.

To be honest with you, I'm kind of relieved. Because at this point, anything that doesn't involve reading sounds pretty good to me.

<u>Tuesday</u>
Me and Rowley racked our brains all day yesterday
trying to figure out how to pay off that eighty-
three dollars. Rowley said maybe I should just go
to the ATM and withdraw some money to pay off
his dad.

The reason Rowley said that is because he thinks
I'm rich. A couple of years ago during the holidays,
Rowley came over and we had just run out of toilet
paper at my house. My family was using these holiday
cocktail napkins as a substitute until Dad got to the
store again.

Rowley thought the holiday napkins were some
kind of really fancy toilet paper, and he asked
me if my family was rich.

I wasn't gonna pass up the opportunity to impress him.

Anyway, I'm NOT rich, and that's the problem. I tried to figure out a way a kid my age could get his hands on some cash, and then it hit me: We could start a lawn care service.

I'm not talking about some average, run-of-the-mill lawn care service, either. I'm talking about a company that takes lawn care to the next level. We decided to name our company the V.I.P. Lawn Service.

We called up the Yellow Pages people and told them we wanted to place an ad in their book. And not just one of those tiny little text ads, but a really big one with full color that takes up two whole pages.

But get this: The Yellow Pages people told us it was gonna cost us a few thousand bucks to put our ad in their book.

I told them that didn't make a lot of sense to me, because how's someone supposed to pay for an ad if they haven't even earned any money yet?

Me and Rowley realized we were gonna have to do this a different way, and make our OWN ads.

I figured we could just make flyers and put them in every mailbox in our neighborhood. All we needed was some clip art to get us started.

So we went down to the corner store and bought one of those cards women get each other on their birthdays.

Then we scanned it into Rowley's computer and pasted pictures of OUR heads onto the bodies from the card.

After that we got some clip art of lawn tools and put it all together. Then we printed it out, and I have to say, it looked great.

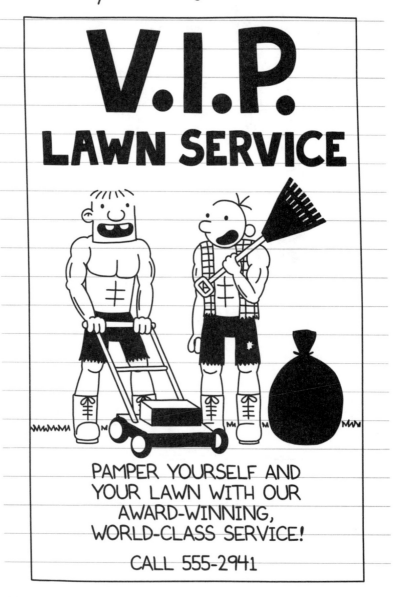

I did some math, and I figured it would cost us at least a couple hundred bucks in color ink cartridges and paper to make enough flyers for the whole neighborhood. So we asked Rowley's dad if he'd go out to the store and get us all the stuff we needed.

Mr. Jefferson didn't go for it. In fact, he told us we couldn't use his computer or print out any more copies of our flyer.

I was a little surprised by that, because if Mr. Jefferson wanted us to pay him back, he sure wasn't making it easy. But all we could really do was take our one flyer and get out of his office.

Then me and Rowley went around from house to house showing everyone our flyer and telling them about the V.I.P. Lawn Service.

After we hit a few houses, we realized it would be a lot easier to just ask the next person we spoke with to pass the flyer along so me and Rowley wouldn't have to do all that walking.

Now the only thing we have to do is sit back and wait for the phone calls to start rolling in.

Thursday
Me and Rowley waited around all day yesterday, but we didn't get any calls.

I was starting to wonder if we should try to find a card with more muscular guys for our next flyer. Then, at about 11:00 this morning, we got a call from Mrs. Canfield, who lives on Gramma's street. She said her lawn needed mowing but she wanted to check our references before she hired us.

I used to do lawn work for Gramma, so I called her up and asked if she could call Mrs. Canfield and tell her what a good worker I am.

Well, I must've caught Gramma on a bad day, because she really lit into me. She said I left piles of leaves on her lawn last fall and now there were patches of dead grass all over her yard.

, she asked me when I was gonna come over finish the job.

That was not really the kind of response I was looking for. I told Gramma we were only taking paying jobs at the moment but maybe we could get back to her later on in the summer.

Then I called Mrs. Canfield and did my best imitation of Gramma. I guess I'm lucky my voice hasn't changed yet.

THE V.I.P. LAWN SERVICE DOES EXCEPTIONAL WORK AND CATERED TO MY EVERY LAWN NEED.

Believe it or not, Mrs. Canfield bought it. She thanked "Gramma" for the reference and hung up. Then she called back a few minutes later, and I answered in my regular voice. Mrs. Canfield said she'd hire us and that we should come by her house later today to get started.

But it's kind of far from my house to Mrs. Canfield's, so I asked her if she could come get us. She didn't seem real happy that we didn't have our own transportation, but she said she'd be willing to pick us up if we could be ready at noon.

Mrs. Canfield came to my house at 12:00 in her son's pickup truck, and she asked us where our lawn mower and all our equipment was.

I said we didn't actually HAVE any equipment but that my Gramma keeps her side door unlocked and I might be able to sneak in and borrow her mower for a few hours. I guess Mrs. Canfield must have been pretty desperate to get her lawn mowed, because she went along with my plan.

Luckily, Gramma wasn't home, so it was easy to get the mower out of her house. We rolled it over to Mrs. Canfield's yard, and then we were ready to get to work.

That's when me and Rowley realized neither one of us had ever actually operated a lawn mower before. So the two of us poked around for a while and tried to figure out how to get the thing started.

Unfortunately, when we tilted the mower on its side, all the gasoline spilled out onto the grass, and we had to go back over to Gramma's to get a refill.

I picked up the owner's manual for the mower while we were at it. I tried to read it, but the instructions were written in Spanish. I got the feeling from the bits and pieces I COULD understand that operating a lawn mower was a lot more dangerous than I originally thought.

PRECAUCIÓN!
El uso incorrecto puede tener como resultado graves lesiones físicas o muerte.

Siempre conserve los pies y las manos alejadas de las cuchillas del cortacésped.

Nunca utilice el cortacésped durante tempestades con truenos.

I told Rowley he could have the first crack at the lawn mowing and that I would go sit in the shade and start working on our business plan.

Rowley didn't like that idea at all. He said this was a "partnership" and that everything had to be 50-50. I was pretty surprised by this, because I'm the one who came up with the idea for the lawn service in the first place, so I was more like the owner than a partner.

I told Rowley we needed someone to do the grunt work and someone to handle the money so it didn't get all sweaty.

Believe it or not, that was enough to make Rowley walk right off the job.

I just wanna say for the record that if Rowley ever needs me for a job reference in the future, I'm gonna have to give him a lousy review.

The truth is, I don't really need Rowley anyway. If this lawn service business grows the way I think it will, I'm gonna have about a HUNDRED Rowleys working for me.

In the meantime, I needed to get Mrs. Canfield's lawn mowed. I looked through the manual for a little while longer and then figured out that I needed to pull on this handle attached to a cord, so I tried that.

The mower started up right away, and I was off and running.

It wasn't as bad as I thought it was gonna
be. The lawn mower was self-propelled, so all I
needed to do was walk behind it and steer every
once in a while.

RRRRR

Then I started to notice that there were
piles of dog poop everywhere. And steering
around them was not an easy thing to do with
a self-propelled mower.

SWERVE

The V.I.P. Lawn Service has a very strict policy
when it comes to dog poop, which is that we won't
go anywhere near it.

So from that point on, whenever I saw anything that looked suspicious, I would mow a ten-foot circle around it just to be safe.

The job actually went a lot faster after that because I had a lot less lawn to cover. After I was done, I went to the front door to collect my money. The final bill was thirty dollars, which was twenty dollars for the lawn plus ten bucks for the time me and Rowley spent designing that flyer.

But Mrs. Canfield wouldn't pay. She said our service was "lousy" and that we hardly mowed any of her lawn.

I told her about the dog poop issue, but she still wouldn't cough up what she owed me. And to make matters worse, she wouldn't even give me a ride home. You know, I figured someone might try to stiff us this summer, but I never thought it would be our very first customer.

I had to walk home, and by the time I got to my house, I was really mad. I told Dad the whole story about my lawn mowing experience and how Mrs. Canfield wouldn't pay me.

Dad drove right over to Mrs. Canfield's house, and I went with him. I thought he was gonna chew her out for taking advantage of his son, and I wanted to be there to see it firsthand. But Dad just got Gramma's mower and cut the rest of Mrs. Canfield's grass.

RRRRRR

When he was done, he didn't even ask her for any money.

The trip wasn't a TOTAL waste of time, though. When Dad wrapped things up, I planted a sign in Mrs. Canfield's front yard.

I figured if I wasn't gonna get paid, I might as well get some free advertising for all my trouble.

Saturday

The V.I.P. Lawn Service has not really panned out the way I thought it would. I haven't had any work since that first job, and I'm starting to think maybe Mrs. Canfield has been bad-mouthing me to her neighbors.

I thought about just giving up and closing our business, but then I realized that with a few tweaks to the flyer, we could start things back up again in the winter.

YOU'VE TRIED THE REST,
NOW GO WITH THE BEST!

The problem is, I need money NOW. I called up
Rowley to start brainstorming new ideas, but his
mom said he was at the movies with his dad. I was
a little annoyed, because he never bothered to ask
me if he could take the day off.

Mom's not letting me do anything fun until this fruit smoothie bill is paid off, so that meant it was up to ME to figure out how to earn the cash.

I'll tell you who has a lot of money, and that's Manny. I mean, that kid is RICH. A few weeks ago Mom and Dad told Manny they'd give him a quarter for every time he uses the potty without being asked. So now he carries around a gallon of water with him at all times.

Manny keeps all his money in a big jar on his dresser. He's gotta have at least $150 in that thing.

I've thought about asking Manny to lend me the money, but I just can't bring myself to do that. I'm pretty sure Manny charges interest on his loans anyway.

I CAN GET THE REST OF IT TO YOU TOMORROW.

I'm trying to figure out a way to earn money without doing any actual work. But when I told Mom what I was thinking, she said I'm just "lazy."

OK, so maybe I AM lazy, but it's not really my fault. I've been lazy ever since I was a little kid, and if someone had caught it early on, maybe I wouldn't be the way I am now.

I remember in preschool, when playtime was over, the teacher would tell everyone to put away their toys, and we would all sing the "Cleanup Song" while we did it. Well, I sang the song with everyone else, but I didn't do any of the actual cleaning.

So if you want to find somebody to blame for the way I am, I guess you'd have to start with the public education system.

Sunday

Mom came into my room this morning and woke me up for church. I was glad to go, because I knew I was gonna have to turn to a higher power to get this fruit smoothie bill paid off. Whenever Gramma needs anything she just prays, and she gets it right away.

I think she has a direct pipeline to God or something.

For some reason I don't have that same kind of pull. But that doesn't mean I'm gonna quit trying.

Today's sermon was called "Jesus in Disguise," and it was about how you should treat everyone you meet with kindness because you never know which person is really Jesus pretending to be someone else.

I guess that's supposed to make you wanna be a better person, but all it does is make me paranoid because I know I'm gonna just end up guessing wrong.

They passed the donation basket around like they do every week, and all I could think was how I needed that money a lot more than whoever it was going to.

But Mom must've seen the look in my eye, because she passed the basket to the row behind us before I could take what I needed.

Monday

My birthday's coming up this weekend, and it can't get here quick enough for me. This year I'm gonna have a FAMILY party. I'm still really burned up with Rowley for bailing out on our lawn care business, so I don't want him thinking he can come over and eat my birthday cake.

Plus, I've learned my lesson about friend parties. When you have a friend party, all your guests think they have the right to play with your presents.

POP

And every time I have a friend party, Mom invites HER friends' kids, so I end up with a bunch of people at my party I barely even know.

And those kids don't buy the gifts, their MOMS do. So even if you get something like a video game, it's not a video game you'd actually want to play.

I'm just glad I'm not on the swim team this summer. Last year I had practice on my birthday, and Mom dropped me off at the pool.

I got so many birthday noogies that I couldn't even lift my arms to swim.

So when it comes to your birthday, I've learned it's best to just keep kids out of the equation.

Mom said I could have a family party as long as I promised not to do my "usual" with the birthday cards. That stinks, because I have a GREAT system for opening cards. I put them all in a neat pile, and then I rip each one open and shake it to get the money out. As long as I don't stop to read anything, I can get through a pile of twenty cards in under a minute.

Mom says the way I do it is "insulting" to the people who got me the cards. She says this time around I have to read every card and acknowledge the person who gave it to me. That'll slow me down, but I guess it's still worth it.

I've been doing a lot of thinking about what I want for my birthday this year. What I REALLY want is a dog.

I've been asking for a dog for the past three years, but Mom says we have to wait until Manny's completely potty trained before we get one. Well, with the potty training racket Manny's got going on, that could take FOREVER.

The thing is, I know that Dad wants a dog, too. He used to have one when HE was a kid.

I figured all Dad needed was a little nudge, and on Christmas last year I saw my chance. My Uncle Joe and his family stopped by our house, and they brought their dog, Killer, with them.

I asked Uncle Joe if he wouldn't mind hinting to Dad that he should get us a dog. But the way Uncle Joe did it probably set my dog-getting campaign back by five years.

The other thing I have no chance of getting for my birthday is a cell phone, and I can thank Rodrick for that.

Mom and Dad got Rodrick a cell phone last year, and he racked up a bill for three hundred dollars in the first month. Most of THAT was from Rodrick calling Mom and Dad from his room in the basement to ask them to turn the heat up.

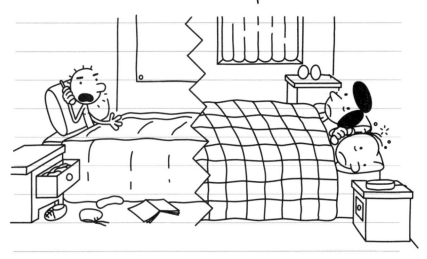

So the only thing I'm asking for this year is a deluxe leather recliner. My Uncle Charlie has one, and he practically LIVES in that thing.

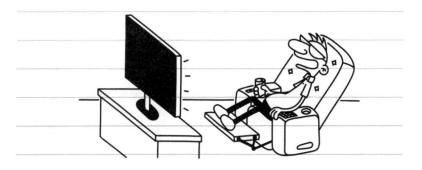

The main reason I want my own recliner is because
if I had one, I wouldn't have to go up to my
room after watching TV late at night. I could
just sleep right in the chair.

Plus, these recliners have all sorts of features, like a
neck massager and adjustable firmness and stuff like
that. I figure I could use the "vibrate" feature to
make Dad's lectures a lot more tolerable.

The only reason I'd ever need to get up is to
go to the bathroom. But maybe I should just
wait until next year to ask for a recliner,
because I bet they'll have that taken care of
in the new model.

Thursday

I asked Mom to take me back to Bombshells
Beauty Salon again today, even though I didn't
really need a haircut. I just felt like catching up
on the town gossip.

Annette, my hairstylist, said she heard from a lady
who knows Mrs. Jefferson that me and Rowley had
a falling out.

Apparently, Rowley's "heartbroken" because I didn't invite him to my birthday party. Well, if Rowley's upset, you wouldn't know it from looking at him.

Every time I see Rowley, he's palling around with his dad. So the way it looks to me, he's already got himself a new best friend.

I just wanna say I think it stinks that Rowley gets to go to the country club even though he still owes money on that fruit smoothie bill.

Unfortunately, Rowley's chummy relationship with his dad is starting to affect MY life. Mom says the way Rowley and his dad hang out together is "neat" and that me and Dad should go fishing or play catch in the front yard or something.

But the thing is, me and Dad just aren't cut out for that kind of father-son stuff. The last time Mom tried to get me and Dad to do something like that together, it ended with me having to pull him out of Rappahannock Creek.

Mom won't let it go, though. She says she wants to see more "affection" between Dad and us boys. And that's created some really awkward moments.

<u>Friday</u>
Today I was watching TV, minding my own
business, when I heard a knock at the front
door. Mom said there was a "friend" there to
see me, so I thought it must be Rowley coming
to apologize.

But it wasn't Rowley. It was FREGLEY.

After I recovered from my initial shock, I
slammed the door shut. I started to panic because
I didn't know what Fregley was doing at my
front door. After a few minutes went by, I
looked out the side window, and Fregley was
STILL standing there.

I knew I had to take drastic measures, so I went to the kitchen to call the cops. But Mom stopped me before I could finish dialing 911.

Mom said SHE invited Fregley over. She said I've seemed "lonely" ever since I had that fight with Rowley, and she thought she'd set up a "playdate" with Fregley.

See, this is why I should never tell Mom about my personal business. This Fregley thing was a total disaster.

I've heard that a vampire can't come inside your house unless you invite him in, and I'll bet it's the same kind of deal with Fregley.

MIND IF I BORROW SOME FLOUR?

SURE, IT'S BACK IN THE KITCH— HEY, **WAIT** A SECOND!

So now I've got TWO things to worry about: the muddy hand and Fregley. And if I had to choose the one to get me first, I'd take the muddy hand in a heartbeat.

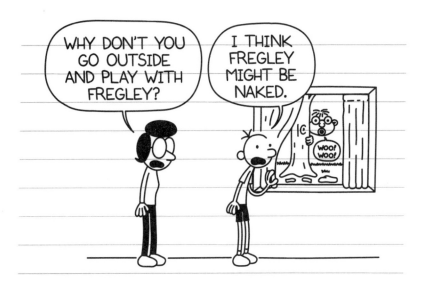

Saturday

Today was my birthday, and I guess things went more or less like I expected. The relatives started showing up around 1:00. I asked Mom to invite as many people as possible so I could maximize my gift potential, and I got a pretty good turnout.

I like to cut to the chase on my birthday and get right to the gifts, so I told everyone to gather in the living room.

I took my time with the cards, just like Mom asked. It was a little painful, but I got a good haul, so it was worth it.

A special greeting
And a "how do you do?"
For a special nephew —
By golly, that's you!

Happy
Birthday!

aunt Brenda

WOW, AUNT BRENDA, THIS IS REALLY NEAT!

WHEN I SAW IT IN THE STORE, I KNEW IT WAS JUST PERFECT!

Unfortunately, as soon as I collected my checks, Mom confiscated the money to pay off Mr. Jefferson.

PLUCK

Then I moved on to the wrapped presents, but there weren't a whole lot of those. The first gift, from Mom and Dad, was small and heavy, which I thought was a good sign. But I was still pretty shocked when I opened it.

When I looked more closely, I found out it wasn't an ordinary cell phone. It was called a "Ladybug." The phone didn't have a keypad on it or anything. It only had two buttons: one to call home and one for emergencies. So it's pretty much useless.

All my other gifts were clothes and other stuff I didn't really need. I was still hoping I might get that recliner, but once I realized there weren't any places Mom and Dad could be hiding a giant leather chair, I gave up looking.

Then Mom told everyone it was time to go into the dining room to have some cake. Unfortunately, Uncle Joe's dog, Killer, had beaten us to it.

I was hoping Mom would go out and get me a new cake, but she just took a knife and cut away the parts the dog didn't touch.

Mom cut me a big piece, but by that point I wasn't really in the mood for cake. Especially not with Killer throwing up little birthday candles under the table.

Sunday
I guess Mom must've felt bad about how my birthday went down, because today she said we could go to the mall and get a "makeup gift."

Mom took Manny and Rodrick along for the ride, and she said they could each pick out something, too, which is totally unfair, because it wasn't THEIR birthday yesterday.

We walked around the mall for a while and ended up in a pet store. I was hoping we could pool our money to buy a dog, but Rodrick seemed to be interested in a different kind of pet.

Mom handed us each a five-dollar bill and told us we could buy whatever we wanted, but five bucks doesn't exactly get you very far in a pet store. I finally settled on this really cool angelfish that's all different colors.

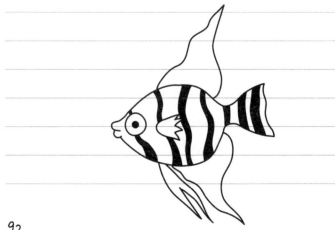

Rodrick picked out a fish, too. I don't know what kind it was, but the reason Rodrick chose it was because the label on the tank said the fish was "aggressive."

Manny spent HIS five bucks on fish food. At first I thought it was because he wanted to feed the fish that me and Rodrick bought, but by the time we got home, Manny had eaten half the canister.

Monday
This is the first time I've had my very own pet, and I'm kind of getting into it. I feed my fish three times a day, and I keep his bowl really clean.

I even bought a journal so I could keep track of everything my fish does during the day. I have to admit, though, I'm starting to have a little trouble filling up the pages.

I asked Mom and Dad if we could buy one of those aquariums and get a ton of fish to keep my little guy company. But Dad said that aquariums cost money and maybe I could ask for one for Christmas.

See, this is what stinks about being a kid. You only get two shots at getting stuff you want, and that's on Christmas and your birthday. And then when one of those days DOES come, your parents mess things up and buy you a Ladybug.

If I had my own money, I could just buy whatever I wanted and not have to embarrass myself every time I needed to rent a video game or buy a piece of candy or something.

Anyway, I've always known that I'll eventually be rich and famous, but I'm starting to get a little concerned that it hasn't happened yet. I figured I'd at LEAST have my own reality TV show by now.

Last night I was watching one of those television shows where a nanny lives with a family for a week and then tells them all the ways they're screwing up.

Well, I don't know if the woman had to go to some special nanny school or something, but that's the kind of job I was BORN to do.

I just need to figure out how to get myself in line for that job when the nanny retires.

YOUR HOUSE IS A WRECK, YOUR KIDS HAVE NO MANNERS, AND...HEY, MR. JOHNSON, YOU'RE NOT GOING OUT IN THAT SHIRT, ARE YOU?

A few years ago I started collecting my personal mementos, like book reports and old toys and stuff like that, because when my museum opens I wanna make sure it's packed with interesting things from my life.

But I don't keep anything like lollipop sticks that have my saliva on them because, believe me, I do NOT need to be cloned.

When I'm famous, I'm gonna have to make some life changes.

I'll probably have to fly in private jets, because if I fly on regular planes, I'll get really annoyed when people in the back try to mooch off my first-class bathroom.

Another thing famous people have to deal with is that their younger siblings end up getting famous just because they're related.

My closest brush with fame so far was when Mom signed me up for a modeling job a few years ago. I think her idea was to get pictures of me in clothes catalogues or something like that.

But the only thing they used my picture for was this stupid medical book, and I've been trying to live it down ever since.

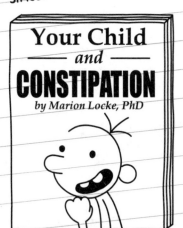

Your Child
— *and* —
CONSTIPATION
by Marion Locke, PhD

<u>Tuesday</u>
I spent the afternoon playing video games and catching up on the Sunday comics.

I turned to the back page, and there was an ad where "Li'l Cutie" usually is.

Man, I've been waiting FOREVER for an opportunity like this. I had a comic in my school paper once, but this is a chance to hit the BIG time.

The ad said they weren't accepting any animal comic strips, and I think I know why. There's this comic about a dog called "Precious Poochie," and it's been running for about fifty years.

The guy who wrote it died a long time ago, but they're still recycling his old comics.

I don't know if they're funny or not because, to be honest with you, most of them don't even make sense to a person my age.

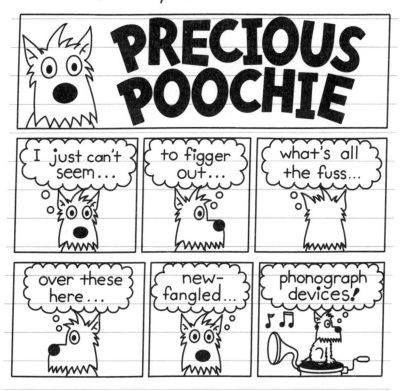

Anyway, the newspaper has tried to get rid of that comic a bunch of times, but whenever they try to cancel it all the "Precious Poochie" fans come out of the woodwork and make a big stink. I guess people think of this cartoon dog as their own pet or something.

The last time they tried to cancel "Precious Poochie," four busloads of senior citizens from Leisure Towers showed up at the newspaper offices downtown and didn't leave until they got their way.

Saturday
Mom was acting extra-cheery this morning, and I could tell she had something up her sleeve.

At 10:00 she said we all needed to get in the station wagon, and when I asked her where we were going, she said it was a "surprise."

I noticed Mom had packed sunscreen and bathing suits and stuff in the back of the station wagon, so I thought we must be headed for the beach.

But when I asked her if I was right, Mom said the place we were going was BETTER than the beach.

Wherever we were going, it was taking a long time to get there. And it wasn't that fun being stuck in the backseat with Rodrick and Manny.

Manny was sitting in between me and Rodrick on the hump. At one point Rodrick decided to tell Manny the hump was the worst seat in the car because it was the smallest and least comfortable.

Well, that totally set Manny off.

Eventually, Mom and Dad got sick of Manny's crying. Mom said I had to take a turn on the hump because I'm the second youngest and it was "only fair." So every time Dad ran over a pothole, my head hit the roof of the car.

At about 2:00 I was getting really hungry, so I asked if we could stop for some fast food. Dad wouldn't pull over, because he said the people at fast-food restaurants are "idiots."

Well, I know why he thinks that. Every time Dad goes to the fried chicken place over near our house, he tries to place his order through the trash can.

I'D LIKE TWO VALUE MEALS AND A BOTTLE OF...HELLO? HELLO?

I saw a sign for a pizza place, and I begged Mom and Dad to let us eat there. But I guess Mom was trying to save money, because she came prepared.

A half hour later we pulled into a big parking lot, and I knew exactly where we were.

We were at the Slipslide Water Park, where we used to go as kids. And I mean LITTLE kids. It's really a place meant for people Manny's age.

Mom must've heard me and Rodrick groan in the backseat. She said we were gonna have a great day as a family and it would be the highlight of our summer vacation.

I have bad memories of the Slipslide Water Park. One time Grandpa took me there, and he left me in the waterslide area for practically the whole day. He said he was gonna go read his book and he'd meet me there in three hours. But I didn't actually go on any slides because of the sign at the entrance.

I thought you had to be forty-eight years old to ride, but it turns out the two little lines next to the number meant "inches."

So I basically wasted my day waiting for Grandpa to come back and get me, and then we had to leave.

Rodrick has bad memories of the Slipslide Water Park, too. Last year his band got booked to do a show on the music stage they have near the wave pool. Rodrick's band asked the park people to set them up with a smoke machine so they could have some special effects for their show.

But somebody screwed up, and they set Rodrick's band up with a BUBBLE machine instead.

I found out the reason Mom took us to the water park today: It was half-price for families. Unfortunately, it looked like just about every family in the state was there, too.

When we got through the gates, Mom rented a stroller for Manny. I convinced her to spend a little more money and rent a double stroller, because I knew it was gonna be a long day and I wanted to conserve my energy.

Mom parked the stroller near the wave pool, which was so crowded you could barely even see the water. After we put on our sunscreen and found a place to sit, I felt a few raindrops, and then I heard thunder. Then an announcement came over the loudspeaker.

DUE TO LIGHTNING, THE SLIPSLIDE WATER PARK IS NOW CLOSED. THANK YOU FOR COMING, AND HAVE A NICE DAY.

Everyone hit the exits and got in their cars. But with all the people trying to leave at the exact same time, it was a total traffic jam.

Manny tried to entertain everyone by telling jokes. At first Mom and Dad were encouraging him.

But after a while, Manny's jokes didn't even make sense.

We were low on gas, so we had to turn off the air conditioner and wait for the parking lot to clear up.

Mom said she had a headache, and she went to the back to lie down. An hour later traffic finally thinned out, and we got onto the highway.

We stopped for gas, and about forty-five minutes later we were home. Dad told me to wake Mom up, but when I looked in the back of the station wagon, Mom wasn't there.

For a few minutes nobody knew where she went. Then we realized the only place she could be was at the gas station. She must've gotten out to use the bathroom when we stopped, and nobody noticed.

Sure enough, that's where she was. We were glad to see her, but I don't think she was too happy to see US.

Mom didn't really say anything on the ride back. Something tells me she's had her fill of family togetherness for a while, and that's good, because I have, too.

Sunday
I really wish we didn't go on that trip yesterday, because if we stayed home, my fish would still be alive.

Before we left for our trip I fed my fish, and Mom said I should feed Rodrick's fish, too. Rodrick's fish was in a bowl on top of the refrigerator, and I'm pretty sure Rodrick hadn't fed his fish or cleaned the bowl once.

I think Rodrick's fish was living off of the algae growing on the glass.

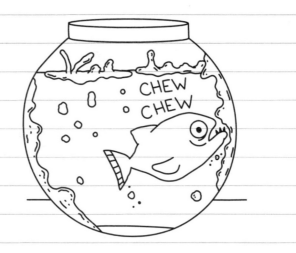

When Mom saw Rodrick's bowl, she thought it was disgusting. So she took his fish and put it in my bowl.

When we got home from the water park, I went straight to the kitchen to feed my fish. But he was gone, and it wasn't a big mystery what happened to him.

I didn't even have time to feel sad about it, because today was Father's Day and we all had to get in the car and go up to Grandpa's for brunch.

I'll tell you this: If I'm ever a dad, you're not gonna see ME dressing up in a shirt and tie and going to Leisure Towers on Father's Day. I'm gonna go off by myself and have some FUN. But Mom said she thought it would be good for the three generations of Heffley men to be together.

I guess I must've been picking at my food, because Dad asked me what was wrong. I told him I was bummed out because my fish died. Dad said he didn't really know what to say because he'd never had a pet die before.

He said he used to have a dog named Nutty when he was a kid, but Nutty ran away to a butterfly farm.

I've heard Dad tell this same story about Nutty and the butterfly farm a million times, but I didn't wanna be rude and cut him off.

Then Grandpa spoke up and said he had a "confession" to make. He said that Nutty didn't actually run away to a butterfly farm. Grandpa said what REALLY happened was that he accidentally ran over the dog when he was backing his car out of the driveway.

Grandpa said he made up the butterfly farm story so he didn't have to tell Dad the truth, but that now they could have a good laugh over it.

But Dad was MAD. He told us to get in the car, and he left Grandpa with the bill for brunch. Dad didn't say anything on the way home. He just dropped us off at the house and drove away.

Dad was gone for a long time, and I was starting to think maybe he was gonna just take the rest of the day for himself. But he showed up an hour later carrying a big cardboard box.

Dad put the box on the floor, and believe it or not, there was a DOG in there.

Mom didn't seem too thrilled that Dad went out and bought a dog without checking with her first. I don't think Dad has ever even bought a pair of pants for himself without getting Mom's OK beforehand. But I think she could see that Dad was happy, so she let him keep it.

At dinner Mom said we should come up with a name for the dog.

I wanted to name it something cool like Shredder or Ripjaw, but Mom said my ideas were too "violent."

Manny's ideas were a whole lot worse, though. He wanted to name the dog an animal name like Elephant or Zebra.

Rodrick liked the animal name idea, and he said we should call the dog Turtle.

Mom said we should call the dog Sweetheart. I thought that was a really terrible idea, because the dog is a BOY, not a girl.

But before any of us could fight it, Dad agreed with Mom's idea.

I think Dad was willing to go with anything Mom came up with if it meant he didn't have to take the dog back. But something tells me Uncle Joe would not approve of our dog's name.

Dad told Rodrick he should go to the mall to buy a bowl and get the dog's name printed on it, and here's what Rodrick came back with —

I guess that's what you get when you send the worst speller in the family off to do your errands.

Wednesday
I was really happy when we got our dog at first, but now I'm starting to have second thoughts.

The dog's actually been driving me crazy. A few nights ago a commercial came on TV, and it showed some gophers popping in and out of their holes. Sweetie seemed pretty interested in that, so Dad said —

WHERE ARE THE GOPHERS, SWEETIE? WHERE ARE THEY, BOY?

That got Sweetie all riled up, and he started barking at the TV.

Now Sweetie barks at the TV CONSTANTLY, and the only thing that gets him to stop is when the commercial with the gophers comes back on.

But what really bugs me about the dog is that he likes to sleep in my bed, and I'm afraid he'll bite my hand off if I try to move him.

And he doesn't just sleep in my bed. He sleeps right smack in the middle.

Dad comes in my room at 7:00 every morning to take Sweetie out. But I guess me and the dog have something in common, because he doesn't like getting out of bed in the morning, either. So Dad turns the lights on and off to try to make the dog wake up.

Yesterday Dad couldn't get Sweetie to go outside, so he tried something new. He went to the front of the house and rang the doorbell, which made the dog shoot out of bed like a rocket.

The only problem was, he used my face as a launching pad.

DING DONG

BARK BARK
BARK BARK

It must've been raining outside this morning, because when Sweetie came back in he was shivering and soaking wet. Then he tried to get under the covers with me to get warm. Luckily, the muddy hand has given me a lot of practice with this sort of thing, so I was able to keep him out.

Thursday

This morning Dad wasn't able to get the dog out of my bed no matter WHAT he tried. So he went to work, and about an hour later Sweetie woke me up to take him outside. I wrapped myself in my blanket and then let the dog out the front door and waited for him to do his business. But Sweetie decided to make a run for it, and I had to chase after him.

You know, I was actually having a pretty decent summer until Sweetie came along. He's ruining the two things that are the most important to me: television and sleep.

And you know how Dad is always getting on my case about lying around all day? Well, Sweetie is twice as bad as me, but Dad's CRAZY about that dog.

I don't think the feeling is mutual, though. Dad is always trying to get the dog to give him a kiss on the nose, but Sweetie won't do it.

I can kind of understand why the dog doesn't like Dad.

The only person Sweetie really likes is Mom, even though she barely pays him any attention. And I can tell that's starting to drive Dad a little nuts.

I think Sweetie is just more of a ladies' man. So I guess that's something else we have in common.

JULY

<u>Saturday</u>

Last night I was working on a new comic to replace "Li'l Cutie." I figured there would be a lot of competition for the open slot, so I wanted to come up with something that really stood out. I made up this comic called "Hey, People!" that's sort of like a half cartoon, half advice column. I figure I can use it to make the world a better place, or at least a better place for ME.

UM...LET'S SEE...I GUESS... HMM...

WHEN ORDERING FROM A FAST-FOOD RESTAURANT, TRY TO DECIDE WHAT YOU WANT <u>BEFORE</u> YOU GET TO THE FRONT OF THE LINE.

I figured since Dad reads the comics, I might as well write a few that were specifically targeted at him.

I would've written a bunch of comics last night, but Sweetie was driving me crazy and I couldn't concentrate.

While I was drawing, the dog was sitting on my pillow licking his paws and his tail, and he was really getting into it.

Whenever Sweetie does that, I have to remember to flip the pillow over when I go to bed. Last night I forgot, and when I lay down I put my head right on the wet spot.

Speaking of licking, Sweetie finally kissed Dad last night. It's probably because Dad had potato chips on his breath, and I think dogs have an automatic response to that sort of thing.

LICK

I didn't have the heart to tell Dad that Sweetie had just spent the past half hour on my pillow licking his rear end.

Anyway, I'm hoping I can write a few more comics tonight, because I'm not gonna be able to get any work done tomorrow. Tomorrow's the Fourth of July, and Mom is making the whole family go to the town pool.

I tried to get out of it, mostly because I want to make it through the summer without having to walk past the shower guys. But I think Mom's still hoping to have one perfect family day this summer, so there's no use fighting it.

Monday

My Fourth of July started out pretty rough. When I got to the pool, I tried to get through the locker room as quickly as I could. But the shower guys were really chatty, and they didn't make it easy on me.

HEY, GREG, HOW'S THE FAMILY?

PATRONS MUST SHOWER BEFORE ENTERING POOL

Then Mom told me she left her sunglasses out in the car, so I had to go BACK through the shower area to the parking lot. I wore Mom's sunglasses on the return trip to make it clear I wasn't interested in conversation, but that didn't work out so good, either.

Seriously, I wish those guys would just take a shower at home before they came to the pool. Because once you see somebody like that, you can never look at them the same way again.

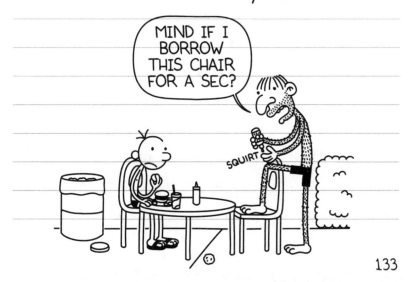

133

After I got past the locker room, things didn't get a whole lot better. The scene was just about how I remembered it, except more crowded. I guess everyone had the same idea to spend the Fourth at the pool.

The only time the pool cleared out was when the lifeguard called a fifteen-minute rest break and all the kids had to get out of the water.

I think the idea behind rest breaks is to give adults a little time to enjoy the pool, but I don't know how they're supposed to relax with three hundred kids waiting for the break to be over.

When I was younger I used to just go swim in the baby pool during the fifteen-minute rest break, but that was before I knew what went on in there.

MAMA, I'M PEEING!

The only area of the pool that wasn't a complete madhouse was the deep end, and that's where the diving boards are. I haven't been in the deep end since I was eight years old, when Rodrick talked me into jumping off the high dive.

Rodrick was always trying to get me to jump off the high dive, but that tall ladder really scared me. He told me I needed to conquer my fears or I'd never become a man.

Then one day Rodrick told me that there was a clown at the top of the diving board who was handing out free toys, and that got my attention.

But by the time I realized Rodrick was full of baloney, it was too late.

Anyway, today Mom got everyone together to go to the picnic area because they were giving out free watermelon.

But I've got a fear of watermelon, too. Rodrick is always telling me that if you eat the seeds, then a watermelon will grow in your stomach.

I don't know if he's telling the truth or not, but school's only a couple of months away, so I'm not willing to take the risk.

When it started getting dark, everyone put their blankets out on the lawn to watch the fireworks display. We sat staring up at the sky for a long time, but nothing was happening.

Then someone came on the loudspeaker and said that the show was canceled because someone left the fireworks out in the rain last night and they got soaked. Some little kids started to cry, so a couple of grown-ups tried to create their own fireworks show.

Luckily, the fireworks display at the country club down the road started right about then. It was a little hard to see over the trees, but at that point I don't think anyone really cared.

Tuesday

This morning I was sitting at the kitchen table
flipping through the comics, and I came across
something that almost made me spit out my cereal.

It was a two-page back-to-school ad, right where
any kid could see it.

I can't believe it's actually LEGAL to run a
back-to-school ad two months before school
starts. Anyone who would do that kind of thing
must really not like kids.

I'm sure back-to-school ads are gonna start popping up all over the place now, and the next thing you know, Mom is gonna be telling me it's time to go clothes shopping. And with Mom, that's an all-day affair.

So I asked Mom if Dad could take me clothes shopping instead, and she said yes. I think she saw it as some kind of father-son bonding opportunity.

But I told Dad he could just go without me and pick out whatever he wanted.

Well, THAT was a dumb move, because Dad did all of his shopping at the pharmacy.

Before I saw that ad, my day was bad enough already. It rained again this morning, so Sweetie tried to get under the covers with me after Dad took him out.

I guess I must've been a little off my game, because the dog found a gap between the blanket and the bed and managed to get through.

And let me tell you, there's nothing more terrifying than being trapped under your covers wearing nothing but underwear with a wet dog crawling all over you.

I was stewing about the dog and that back-to-
school ad when my whole day turned around. Mom
had printed out some pictures from the Fourth,
and she left them lying on the kitchen table.

In one of the pictures you could see a lifeguard in
the background. It was a little hard to tell, but
I'm pretty sure the lifeguard was Heather Hills.

It was so crowded at the pool yesterday that I didn't even notice the lifeguards. And if that really WAS Heather Hills, I can't believe I missed her.

Heather Hills is the sister of Holly Hills, who is one of the cutest girls in my class. But Heather's in HIGH school, which is a whole different league than middle school.

HEATHER HILLS

HOLLY HILLS

This Heather Hills thing is changing my whole perspective on the town pool. In fact, I'm starting to rethink my whole SUMMER. The dog has ruined all the fun of being at home, and I realized that if I don't do something quick, I won't have anything good to say about my vacation.

So starting tomorrow I'm gonna have a whole new attitude. And hopefully by the time I get back to school, I'll have a high school girlfriend, too.

Wednesday

Mom was really happy I was willing to go to the pool with her and Manny today, and she said she was proud I was finally putting my family in front of video games. I didn't mention Heather Hills to Mom, because I don't need her getting in the middle of my love life.

When we got there, I wanted to go straight to the pool area and see if Heather was on duty. But then I realized I'd better be prepared in case she was.

So I made a pit stop in the bathroom and lathered myself in suntan oil. Then I did a bunch of push-ups and sit-ups to really make my muscles pop.

I was probably in there for about fifteen minutes. I was checking myself out in the mirror when I heard someone in a stall clear his throat.

AHEM.

Well, that was pretty embarrassing, because it meant whoever was in there could see me flexing in front of the mirror the whole time. And if that person was anything like ME, he couldn't go to the bathroom until he had complete privacy.

I figured the person in the stall couldn't see my face, so at least he didn't know who I was. I was just about to slip out of the bathroom when I heard Mom at the front of the locker room.

GREG? GREGORY HEFFLEY? ARE YOU STILL IN THERE?

Mom wanted to know what took me so long and why I looked so "shiny," but I was already looking past her and scanning the lifeguard stands to see if Heather Hills was on deck.

And sure enough, she was. I went right over to her and parked myself underneath her chair.

Every once in a while I'd say something witty, and I think I was definitely impressing her.

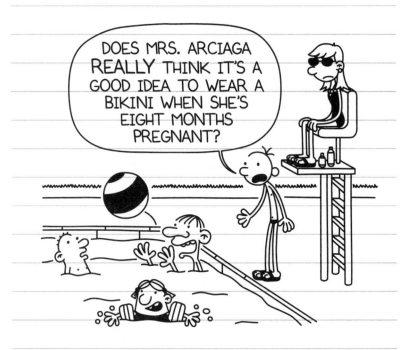

DOES MRS. ARCIAGA REALLY THINK IT'S A GOOD IDEA TO WEAR A BIKINI WHEN SHE'S EIGHT MONTHS PREGNANT?

I'd get Heather a new cup of water whenever it looked like she needed a refill, and every time some kid would do something wrong, I'd speak up so Heather didn't have to.

Whenever Heather's shift ended, I'd follow her to her next station. Every fourth time, I'd end up in front of where Mom was sitting. And let me tell you, it's not easy to be smooth when your mother is sitting five feet away.

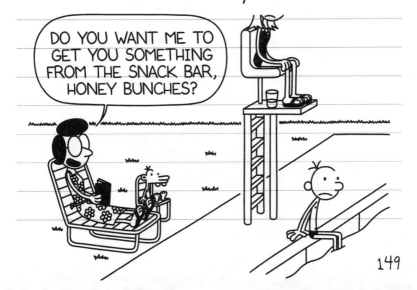

I just hope Heather knows that I would do ANYTHING for her. If she wants someone to put suntan lotion on her back or towel her off after she takes a dip in the pool, I'm the man for the job.

I basically hung out with Heather until it was time to go. On my way home I was thinking that if the rest of my vacation goes like today, this WILL be the best summer ever, just like Mom predicted. In fact, the only thing that can ruin things now is that stupid muddy hand. I'm sure it'll show up at the exact wrong moment and spoil everything.

GREG HEFFLEY, DO YOU TAKE HEATHER HILLS TO BE YOUR LAWFULLY WEDDED WIFE?

TAP TAP

<u>Wednesday</u>

I've been hanging out with Heather every single day for the past week.

I realized my friends at school will never believe it when I tell them about me and Heather, so I asked Mom to take a picture of me standing next to the lifeguard chair.

Mom didn't have her camera, so she had to use her cell phone. But she couldn't figure out how to take a picture with it, and I ended up standing there for a long time looking like a fool.

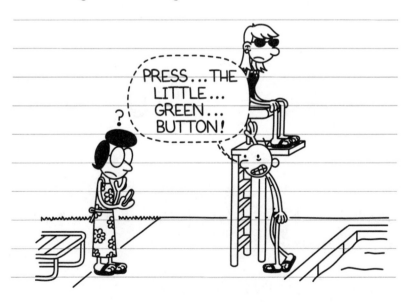

PRESS...THE LITTLE... GREEN... BUTTON!

I finally got Mom to press the right button to take a picture, but when she did, the camera was pointed the wrong way and she took a picture of herself. See, this is why I always say that technology is wasted on grown-ups.

I got Mom to point the camera at me, but right at that moment her phone rang and she answered it.

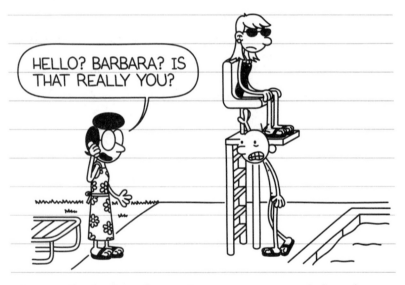

HELLO? BARBARA? IS THAT REALLY YOU?

Mom talked for about five minutes, and by the time she was done, Heather was on to her next shift. But that didn't stop Mom from taking the picture anyway.

<u>Friday</u>
Relying on Mom for my ride to the pool is starting
to become a problem. Mom doesn't want to go to
the pool every day, and when she DOES go, she
only stays a few hours.

I like to be at the pool from the time it opens
until the time it closes so I can maximize my
time with Heather. I wasn't about to ask
Rodrick to drive me to the pool in his van
because he always makes me sit in the back, and
there are no seats.

I realized I need my OWN transportation,
and luckily I found a solution yesterday.

One of our neighbors left a bike out by the curb, and I took it before anyone else could.

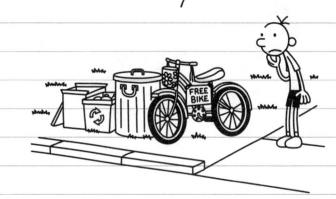

I rode the bike home and parked it in the garage. When Dad saw it, he said it was a "girl bike" and I should get rid of it.

But I'll tell you at least two reasons a girl bike is better than a boy bike. Number one, girl bikes have big, cushiony seats, and that's really important when you're riding in your bathing suit.

GIRL SEAT

BOY SEAT

And number two, girl bikes have those baskets on the handlebars, which are good for carrying your video games and suntan lotion. Plus, my bike came with a bell, and that REALLY comes in handy.

Monday
I guess I should've known that a bike that was left out with the trash wasn't gonna last very long.

I was riding home from the pool yesterday, and the bike started getting all wobbly. Then the front wheel popped right off. So today I had to ask Mom for a ride to the pool.

When we got there, Mom said I had to take Manny with me through the locker room. She said he's getting too old to go through the women's locker room with her, so I guess they must have the same shower situation in there as they do in the men's locker room.

It should've taken about five seconds to get Manny from one end of the locker room to the other, but it took about ten minutes instead.

Manny goes everywhere with Mom, so he had never actually BEEN in a men's bathroom before. He was really curious and wanted to check everything out. At one point I had to stop him from washing his hands in the urinal because I guess he thought it was a sink.

I didn't want Manny to have to walk through the shower area and see the things I've seen. So I got a towel out of my bag and was gonna put it over Manny's eyes when we walked past the shower guys. But in the two seconds it took me to get my towel, Manny was gone. And you'll never believe where he went.

I knew I had to rescue Manny, so I closed my eyes as tight as I could and went in to save him.

I was really nervous about touching one of the
shower guys, and for a second there I thought
I did.

I had to open my eyes to find Manny, and then I
grabbed him and got out as fast as I could.

When we got to the other side, Manny seemed
fine, but I don't think I'll ever totally recover
from that experience.

I kind of staggered over to my spot underneath Heather's lifeguard chair. Then I started taking deep breaths to calm myself down.

Five minutes later some kid who must've eaten too much ice cream threw up behind Heather's chair. Heather looked behind her, and then she looked down like she was waiting for me to do something. I guess the noble thing to do was to clean up the mess for Heather, but this was really beyond the call of duty.

Anyway, I've been doing a lot of thinking lately, and I've realized that I need to let this summer romance cool off a little.

Plus, Heather's going off to college next year, and those long-distance relationships never really seem to work out.

AUGUST

<u>Tuesday</u>
We ran into the Jeffersons at the supermarket today. Me and Rowley haven't spoken to each other in over a month, so it was kind of awkward.

Mrs. Jefferson said they were buying groceries for their trip to the beach next week. That kind of irritated me because that's where MY family was supposed to go this summer. But then Mrs. Jefferson said something that really threw me for a loop.

HOW WOULD GREGORY LIKE TO **JOIN** US?

Mr. Jefferson didn't look too thrilled with that idea, but before he could speak up Mom chimed in.

WHY, GREGORY WOULD LOVE TO!

Something about the whole incident seemed a little fishy to me. I'm kind of wondering if it was a setup, with Mom and Mrs. Jefferson conspiring to get me and Rowley back together.

Believe me, Rowley's the LAST person I want to spend a week with. But then I realized if I went to the beach with the Jeffersons, I'd get to ride the Cranium Shaker. So maybe my summer won't be such a bust after all.

Monday
I knew I made a mistake coming on this beach trip when I saw where we were staying.

QUIET
COVE

My family always rents a condo in the high-rises right near the boardwalk, but the place where the Jeffersons are staying is a log cabin about five miles from the beach. We went inside the cabin, and there was no TV or computer or ANYTHING with a screen on it.

I asked what we were supposed to do for entertainment, and Mrs. Jefferson said —

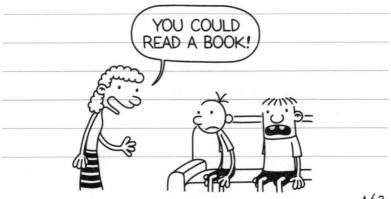

I thought that was a good one, and I was about to tell Rowley his mom was pretty funny. But she came back a second later with a bunch of reading material.

So that just CONFIRMED Mom was in on this plan from the beginning.

All three Jeffersons read their books right up until it was time to eat. Dinner was OK, but dessert was awful. Mrs. Jefferson is one of those moms who sneaks healthy food into your snacks, and her brownies were full of spinach.

I don't think it's a good idea to grind up vegetables and put them in kids' desserts, because then they don't know what the real thing is supposed to taste like.

The first time Rowley had a regular brownie was at my house, and believe me, it wasn't pretty.

After dinner Mrs. Jefferson called us all into the living room to play games. I was hoping we were gonna play something normal like cards, but the Jeffersons have their own idea of fun.

The Jeffersons played a game called "I Love You Because," and when it was my turn, I passed.

Then we played charades, and when it was Rowley's turn, he was a dog.

At about 9:00 Mr. Jefferson told us it was time for bed. That's when I found out the sleeping situation at the Jeffersons' cabin was worse than the entertainment situation.

There was only one bed, so I told Rowley we could make a deal: We'd flip a coin, and one guy would get the bed and the other would sleep on the floor.

But Rowley took a look at the crusty shag carpet and decided he didn't want to risk it. I decided I wasn't willing to sleep on the floor, either. So I got into bed with Rowley and just stayed as far away from him as possible.

Rowley started snoring right away, but I was having trouble falling asleep with half my body hanging off the bed. I was finally starting to drift off when Rowley let out a scream like he was being attacked.

For a second there I thought the muddy hand had finally caught up with us.

Rowley's parents came running in to see what happened.

Rowley said he had a nightmare that there was a chicken hiding underneath him.

So Rowley's parents spent the next twenty minutes trying to calm him down and telling him it was just a bad dream and there really was no chicken.

Nobody bothered to check on how I was doing after falling off the bed onto my face.

Rowley spent the rest of the night sleeping in his parents' room, which was fine with me. Because without Rowley and his chicken dreams to keep me awake, I was able to get a good night's sleep.

Wednesday
I've been stuck inside this cabin for three days now, and I'm really starting to lose my mind.

I've been trying to get Mr. and Mrs. Jefferson to take us to the boardwalk, but they say it's too "noisy" there.

I've never gone this long without TV or computers or video games, and I'm starting to feel kind of desperate. When Mr. Jefferson works late at night on his laptop, I sneak downstairs and watch him just to get a glimpse of the outside world.

I've tried to get Mr. Jefferson to let me use his laptop a couple of times, but he says it's his "work computer" and he doesn't want me to mess anything up. Last night I was at my breaking point, so I did something a little risky.

When Mr. Jefferson got up to use the bathroom,
I jumped at my chance.

I rattled off an e-mail to Mom as quick as I
could, then ran upstairs and got into bed.

TO: Heffley, Susan
SUBJECT: SOS

HELP HELP GET ME OUT OF HERE THESE
PEOPLE ARE DRIVING ME CRAZY

When I came downstairs for breakfast this morning,
Mr. Jefferson didn't look too happy to see me.

It turns out that I sent that e-mail from Mr. Jefferson's work account, and Mom answered back.

TO: Jefferson, Robert
SUBJECT: RE: SOS

Family vacations can be a challenge! Is Gregory not behaving himself?

- Susan

I thought Mr. Jefferson was gonna really let me have it, but he didn't say anything at all. Then Mrs. Jefferson said maybe we could go to the boardwalk later on this afternoon and spend an hour or two there.

Well, that's all I was ever asking for. A few hours is all I really need.

If I can just ride the Cranium Shaker once, I'll feel like this trip wasn't a total waste of time.

Friday
I'm back home from the beach two days early, and if you wanna know the reason why, it's kind of a long story.

The Jeffersons took me and Rowley to the boardwalk yesterday afternoon. I wanted to go on the Cranium Shaker right away, but the line was too long, so we decided to get some food and come back later.

We got some ice cream, but Mrs. Jefferson only ordered one cone for the four of us to share.

WANT A LICK?

Mom gave me thirty dollars to spend at the beach, and I blew twenty of it on this one carnival game.

I was trying to win a giant stuffed caterpillar, but I think they have those games rigged so you can't succeed.

Rowley watched me blow my twenty dollars, and then he asked his dad to buy him the EXACT same giant caterpillar at a shop next door. And the thing that really stinks is that it only cost him ten bucks.

I think Mr. Jefferson is making a big mistake with a move like that. Now Rowley feels like a winner even though he isn't.

I've had my own experience with that sort of thing. Last year when I was on the swim team, they had this special swim meet I got invited to on a Sunday.

When I showed up, I realized none of the GOOD swimmers were there. It was only the kids who had never won a ribbon before.

At first I was pretty happy, because I thought I might actually WIN something for once.

I still didn't do well, though. My event was the 100-meter freestyle, and I got so pooped that I had to WALK the last lap.

But the judges didn't disqualify me. And at the end of the night, I got a first-place ribbon, which my parents handed to me.

In fact, EVERYONE walked away with first-place ribbons, even Tommy Lam, who got turned around in the backstroke and swam the wrong way.

When I got home, I was confused. But then Rodrick saw me with my first-place Champions ribbon, and he gave me the scoop.

Rodrick told me the Champions meet is just a scam put on by parents to make their kids feel like winners.

I guess parents think they're doing their kids a favor by going through with all that, but if you ask me, I think it just causes more problems down the road.

I remember when I used to be on the tee-ball team and everyone would cheer even when I struck out. Then the next year, in junior baseball, all my teammates and the other parents would boo me off the field if I dropped a pop fly or something.

All I'm saying is, if Rowley's parents wanna make him feel good about himself, they can't do it now when he's a kid and then walk away. They've gotta stick with him all the way through.

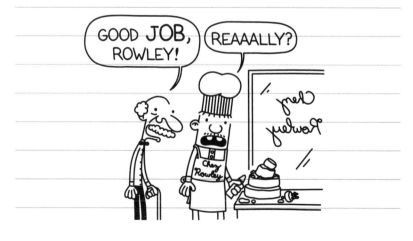

After the caterpillar thing we just walked up and down the boardwalk, waiting for the line for the Cranium Shaker to go down. Then I saw something that got my attention.

It was that girl from Rodrick's keychain picture. But here's the thing: She wasn't a real person. She was a CARDBOARD CUTOUT.

I felt like an idiot for ever thinking that she was a real girl. Then I realized I could buy my OWN keychain picture and impress all the guys at school. I might even be able to make some money by charging them to look at it.

I paid my five bucks and posed for my photo. Unfortunately, the Jeffersons got into the picture WITH me, so now my souvenir keychain is pretty much worthless.

I was really mad, but I forgot all about it when I saw that the line for the Cranium Shaker was down to a few people. I ran over to the ride and used my last five dollars to pay for a ticket.

I thought Rowley was right behind me, but he was hanging back about ten feet. I guess he was too scared to go on.

I was starting to have second thoughts myself, but it was too late. After the ride operator strapped me in, he locked the cage and I knew there was no turning back.

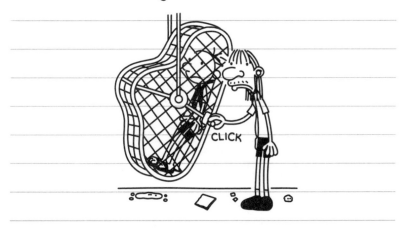

CLICK

Well, I wish I had spent more time watching what the Cranium Shaker actually DID to a person, because I never would've gotten on if I had.

It flips you upside down about a million times and then throws you toward the ground so your face is about six inches from the pavement. Then it sends you spinning backward up to the sky again.

And the whole time the cage you're in is creaking, and all the bolts look like they're about to come loose. I tried to get someone to stop the ride, but nobody could hear me over the pounding heavy metal music.

It was the most nauseous I've ever felt in my life. And when I say that, I mean even more than after I had to get Manny out of the shower area at the town pool. If this is what it takes to be a "man," I am definitely not ready yet.

When the ride finally ended, I could barely walk. So I sat down on a bench and waited for the boardwalk to stop spinning.

I stayed there a long time and focused on trying not to throw up, while Rowley rode some rides that were more his speed.

After Rowley was done with his kiddie rides, his dad bought him a boppy balloon and a shirt from the souvenir shop.

A half hour later I was finally ready to try standing up and walking around again. But when I got on my feet, Mr. Jefferson said it was time to go.

I asked him if we could just play a few games in the arcade, and he said OK even though he didn't seem happy about it.

I had spent all the money Mom gave me, so I told Mr. Jefferson twenty dollars would probably do it. But all he was willing to offer me was a dollar.

I think the arcade was too loud for Mr. and Mrs. Jefferson, so they didn't want to go inside. They told us to go in by ourselves and meet them outside in ten minutes.

I went to the back of the arcade, where they have this game called Thunder Volt. I spent about fifty dollars on that game last year, and I got the high score. I wanted Rowley to see my name at the top of the list, because I wanted to show him what it was like to win something without it being handed to you.

Well, my name was still at the top of the list, but the person who got the NEXT highest score must've been jealous they couldn't beat me.

```
╔══════════════════════════════╗
║        HIGH SCORES           ║
║  ─────────────────────────   ║
║  1. GREG HEFFLEY ....... 25320║
║  2. IS AN IDIOT ........ 25310║
║  3. JARHEAD 71 ......... 24200║
║  4. RECKLESS ........... 22100║
║  5. CRAVEN1 ............ 21500║
║  6. POKECHIMP88 ........ 21250║
║  7. WILD DOG ........... 21200║
║  8. ZIPPY .............. 20300║
║  9. SNARL CARL ......... 20100║
║  10. LEIGHANDREW ....... 19250║
╚══════════════════════════════╝
```

I unplugged the machine to try and wipe out the high scores, but they were burned into the screen permanently.

I was gonna just spend our money on some other game, but then I remembered a trick Rodrick told me about, and I realized we could make the dollar last a lot longer.

Me and Rowley walked outside and went underneath the boardwalk. Then I slipped the dollar bill up between the planks of wood and waited for our first victim.

Eventually, a teenager spotted the dollar sticking out of the boardwalk.

When he went to grab it, I pulled the dollar bill through the slat at the last second.

I have to hand it to Rodrick, because this was actually a lot of fun.

The teenagers we pranked weren't too happy, though, and they came after us. Me and Rowley ran as fast as we could, and we didn't stop until we were pretty sure we shook those guys.

But I STILL didn't feel safe. I asked Rowley to show me some of the moves he learned in karate so we could handle those guys if they found us.

But Rowley said he's a gold belt in karate and he wasn't going to teach his moves to a "no belt."

We hid there a while more, but the teenagers never showed up, and eventually we decided the coast was clear. That's when we realized we were underneath Kiddie Land, so there was a whole new batch of victims for our dollar bill trick right above our heads. And we got a MUCH better reaction out of those kids than we did from the teenagers.

But one of the kids was really fast, and he grabbed the dollar before I could pull it down. So me and Rowley had to go up on the boardwalk to get it back.

This kid wasn't budging, though. I tried to explain the concept of personal property to him, but he STILL wouldn't give us our money.

I was getting pretty frustrated with this kid, and that's when Rowley's parents showed up. I was pretty glad to see them because I figured if ANYONE could talk some sense into this kid, it was Mr. Jefferson.

But Mr. Jefferson was mad, and I mean REALLY mad. He said he and Mrs. Jefferson had been looking all over for us for the past hour and they were ready to call the police to report us missing.

Then he told us we had to get in the car. But on the way to the parking lot, we walked past the arcade. I asked Mr. Jefferson if we could please have another dollar since we never did get to spend that one he gave us.

But I guess that wasn't the right thing to ask, because he took us back to the car without saying a word.

When we got back to the cabin, Mr. Jefferson said me and Rowley had to go straight to our room. That really stunk, because it wasn't even 8:00 and it was still light outside.

But Mr. Jefferson said we had to go to bed and that he didn't want to hear a peep out of us until morning. Rowley was taking it really hard. From the way he was acting, I don't think he's ever been in trouble with his dad before.

I decided to lighten the mood a little bit. I walked around on the shag carpet and then gave Rowley a static electricity shock as a joke.

That seemed to get Rowley to snap out of it. He walked around in a circle for about five minutes rubbing his feet on the carpet, and then got me back while I was brushing my teeth.

I couldn't let Rowley one-up me like that, so when he got into bed I got his boppy balloon, pulled back the giant rubber band, and let it rip.

If I had to do it again, maybe I wouldn't have pulled back so hard.

When Rowley saw the red mark on his arm he screamed, and I knew that was gonna attract attention. Sure enough, his parents were up in our room in five seconds.

I tried to explain that the mark on Rowley's arm was from a rubber band, but that didn't seem to matter to the Jeffersons.

They called my parents, and two hours later Dad was at the cabin to pick me up and take me home.

Monday
Dad's really mad that he had to drive four hours round-trip to come get me. But Mom wasn't mad at all. She said the incident between me and Rowley was just "horseplay" and she was glad we were "pals" again.

But Dad is still mad, and it's been really chilly between us ever since we got back. Mom's been trying to get the two of us to do something like go to the movies together so we can "make peace," but I think right now it's best for me and Dad to just stay out of each other's way.

I think Dad's bad mood is here to stay, though, and part of it has nothing to do with me. When I opened up today's paper, here's what I saw in the Arts section—

Arts

Beloved comic to continue

"Li'l Cutie" to be carried on by original cartoonist's son

In a stunning development, Tyler Post, the son of "Li'l Cutie" cartoonist Bob Post, will take up the pen and carry on his father's enduring one-panel comic.

"I didn't really have a job or any big plans, so one day I said, 'How hard can it be?'" said Tyler, who, at 32, is living with his father. It is widely believed that the Li'l Cutie character is based

See **CUTIE**, page A2

Tyler Post will pen new "Li'l Cutie" comics, the first of which will appear in the paper a week from Sunday.

Related: Leisure Towers residents rejoice, page A3

Last night Dad came into my room and talked to me, which was the first time we spoke to each other in about three days. He said he wanted to make sure I was around on Sunday, and I said I would be.

Later on I heard him talking to someone on the phone, and he seemed to be acting kind of secretive.

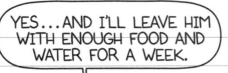

After that I asked Dad if he was taking me anywhere in particular on Sunday, and that seemed to make him really uncomfortable. He said no, but he wouldn't look me in the eye.

Now I knew Dad wasn't telling the truth, so I started to get kind of worried. Dad was willing to ship me off to a military academy before, and I wouldn't put anything past him.

I didn't know what to do, so I told Rodrick what was going on and asked him if he had any theories about what Dad was up to. He told me he'd think about it, and a little while later he came up to my room and shut the door.

Rodrick told me he thought Dad was so mad about the Rowley thing that he was gonna get rid of me.

I wasn't sure if I believed him, because Rodrick's not always 100% reliable. But Rodrick told me if I didn't believe him I should go check out Dad's day planner and see for myself. So I went into Dad's office and opened his calendar to Sunday, and here's what I found —

I'm pretty sure Rodrick was pulling my leg, because it looked an awful lot like his handwriting. But Dad's kind of an unpredictable guy, so I guess I'll just have to wait until Sunday to know for sure.

Sunday
The good news is Dad didn't sell me or give me away to an orphanage today. The bad news is, after what happened, he probably will.

At about 10:00 this morning, Dad said to get in the car because he wanted to take me into the city. When I asked what for, he said it was a "surprise."

SHUDDER

On the way into the city we stopped for gas. Dad had left a map and directions on the dashboard of the car, so now I knew where we were going: 1200 Bayside Street.

Well, I was pretty desperate, so for the first time ever I used my Ladybug.

I finished my call right before Dad came back to the car, and we headed into the city. I just wish I took a better look at that map, because when we pulled up to Bayside Street, I realized it was the parking lot for the baseball stadium. But by then it was too late.

It turns out Mom had bought us tickets to the baseball game for some special father-son bonding and Dad was trying to keep it a surprise.

But it took Dad a long time to explain all of
that to the cops. After he cleared things up
with the police, Dad wasn't in the mood for a
baseball game, so he just took me home.

I felt kind of bad because the seats Mom got us
were in the third row, and it looked to me like
they cost a fortune.

<u>Tuesday</u>

I finally found out what that phone call was all
about the other day. Dad had been on the phone
with Gramma, and they were talking about Sweetie,
not me.

Mom and Dad had decided to give the dog to
Gramma, and Dad dropped Sweetie off on
Sunday night. To be honest with you, I don't
think anyone's really gonna miss him around here.

Me and Dad haven't talked to each other since
then, and I've been looking for excuses to stay
out of the house. I found a really good one
yesterday. There was a commercial on TV for
this store called the Game Hut, which is where
I buy all my video games.

They're having a competition where you play at your local store, and if you win you get to advance to the national playoffs. And the winner of THAT gets a million bucks.

The competition at my local store is on Saturday. I'm sure there are gonna be a ton of people at that thing, so I'm gonna go super early to make sure I get a good place in line.

I learned that trick from Rodrick. Whenever he wants to get tickets to a concert, he camps out the night before. In fact, that's where he met his band's lead singer, Bill.

Rowley and his dad go camping all the time, so I knew he had a tent. I called Rowley and told him about the video game contest and how we could win a million bucks.

But Rowley was acting nervous on the phone. I think he was still worried that I had electrical superpowers or something, and the only way to get him to calm down was to promise I wouldn't use them on him.

Even after we were past that, Rowley didn't seem comfortable with the campout idea. He said his mom and dad banned him from seeing me for the rest of the summer.

I pretty much figured that, but I had a plan to get around it. I told Rowley that I'd tell my parents I was going up to his house to spend the night, and he could tell his parents he was going to Collin's.

Rowley STILL didn't seem sure, so I told him I'd bring him his very own box of gummy bears if he came along, and that sold him.

Saturday
Last night we met at the top of the hill at 9:00. Rowley brought the camping equipment and the sleeping bag, and I brought the flashlight and some chocolate energy bars.

I didn't have the gummy bears right at that moment, but I promised Rowley I'd buy him some the first chance I got.

When we got to the Game Hut we were the only people there, and I couldn't believe our luck.

So we pitched our tent in front of the store before anyone else could take our spot.

Then we watched the door to make sure no one tried to cut in front of us.

I figured the best way to save our place in line was to sleep in shifts. I even offered to take the first shift and let Rowley sleep, because that's just the kind of person I am.

After my shift was over I woke Rowley up for his turn, but he fell back asleep in about five seconds. So I shook him awake and told him he needed to stay alert.

Rowley didn't even bother trying to defend himself.

I decided it was up to ME to make sure nobody got in front of us, so I stayed up all night. I was starting to have trouble keeping my eyes open around 9:00 in the morning, and I ate both of the energy bars I packed to keep myself going.

I got chocolate all over my hands, and that gave me an idea. I opened the tent flap, then slipped my hand inside and made it crawl like a spider.

I thought it would be funny to make Rowley
think it was the muddy hand. I didn't hear any
noises coming from inside the tent, so I thought
Rowley was still sleeping. But before I had a
chance to open the flap and check, my hand got
crushed to smithereens.

I pulled my hand out of the tent, and my thumb
was already starting to turn purple.

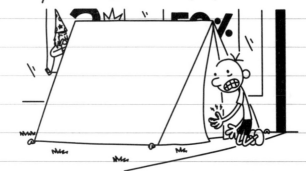

I was really ticked off at Rowley. Not because
he smashed my hand with a mallet, but because
he thought that it could stop the muddy hand.

Any fool knows you have to either use fire or acid to stop a muddy hand. All a mallet's gonna do is make it angry.

I was about to give Rowley a piece of my mind, but right then the guy from the Game Hut came and opened the front door. I tried to ignore the throbbing pain in my thumb and focus on the reason we came here.

The Game Hut guy wanted to know why we had a tent in front of the store, so I told him we were there to compete in the video game contest. But he didn't even know what I was talking about.

So I had to show him the poster from the window to get him up to speed.

The clerk said the store wasn't really set up for a video game tournament but since there were only two of us, maybe we could just play each other in the back room.

I was a little irritated at first, but then I realized all I needed to do to win this tournament was to beat Rowley. So the clerk set us up to play a death match in Twisted Wizard. I almost felt sorry for Rowley, because I'm pretty much an expert at that game. But when we started to play, I realized my thumb was so messed up I couldn't press the buttons on the controller.

All I could do was run around in circles while
Rowley shot me over and over.

Rowley ended up beating me 15-0. The clerk
told Rowley he won the competition and had a
choice: He could either fill out the paperwork to
go to the national tournament, or he could get a
giant box of chocolate-covered raisins.

I'll bet you can guess which one Rowley picked.

Sunday

You know, I should have just stuck with my original plan and stayed inside this summer, because all my trouble started the minute I stepped out of the house.

I haven't seen Rowley since he stole that video game competition from me, and Dad hasn't spoken to me since I almost got him arrested.

But I think things started to turn around for me and Dad today. You remember that article about how "Li'l Cutie" was being passed on from the father to his son?

Well, the son's first comic came out in the paper today, and it looks like the new "Li'l Cutie" is gonna be even worse than the original.

Daddy, can you make my
hiccups hic-DOWN?

I showed Dad, and he agreed with me.

That's when I realized things are gonna be OK between the two of us. Me and Dad might not agree on everything, but at least we agree on the important stuff.

I guess some people would say that hating a comic is a pretty flimsy foundation for a relationship, but the truth is me and Dad hate LOTS of the same things.

Me and Dad might not have one of those close father-son relationships, but that's fine with me. I've learned that there is such a thing as TOO close.

I realized vacation was pretty much over when Mom finished up with her photo album today. I flipped through it, and to be honest with you, I don't think it was a very accurate record of our summer. But I guess the person who takes the pictures is the one who gets to tell the story.

"Best Summer Ever!"

The "Reading Is Fun" gang says "no" to video games.

Now Gregory can't <u>stop</u> reading!

Gregory plays a game of hide 'n' seek with a summer pal.

ACKNOWLEDGMENTS

Thanks to all the fans of the *Wimpy Kid* series for inspiring and motivating me to write these stories. Thanks to all of the booksellers across the nation for putting my books in kids' hands.

Thanks to my family for all the love and support. It's been fun to share this experience with you.

Thanks to the folks at Abrams for working hard to make sure this book happened. A special thanks to Charlie Kochman, my editor; Jason Wells, my publicist; and Scott Auerbach, managing editor extraordinaire.

Thanks to everyone in Hollywood for working so hard to bring Greg Heffley to life, especially Nina, Brad, Carla, Riley, Elizabeth, and Thor. And thanks, Sylvie and Keith, for your help and guidance.

ABOUT THE AUTHOR

Jeff Kinney is an online game developer and designer, and a #1 *New York Times* bestselling author. In 2009, Jeff was named one of *Time* magazine's 100 Most Influential People in the World. He spent his childhood in the Washington, D.C., area and moved to New England in 1995. Jeff lives in southern Massachusetts with his wife and their two sons.